THE LOVE STORY OF DISTANCE

ARCHI SHUKLA

ISBN 979-888530270-8

This one is for love that has taught me how to be me.

Contents

Foreword

The Love Story of Distance is heartwork that reaches every corner of your heart and soul. You will connect with every nook and corner of the masterpiece and really want it to go on and on and on. The book is romantic yet realistic to the very core.

I can never forget the day when this little girl Archi texted me that she's writing a book and sent me just a short snippet.... I was mesmerized by the way she has written it so simply yet beautifully and instantly fell in love with the book.

Writing a book is hard, even for those who do it all the time. And for the less frequent practitioners- they usually get stuck in an awkward passage or in the middle of a sentence, thinking "What's wrong with me?" "Is it good enough?"

But Archi and everyone else, let me tell you...

This book is bloody good enough!!!

-Cadet

Preface

It's truly said that with a vision you can do it all and so it happened.With a vision all you need is a planner that gets you to your destination.This book has lived all of the moments to the fullest soaked with the memories that life showers us.Sometimes all we really need is that courage to stand against the even to be that odd one.This book came to existence only because of the situations that happened in the past that inspired me to be a part of the change through my experiences,that will be a part of someone's survival in the present as well as in the future too.With constant efforts and perseverance everything can be made possible,all that one needs is that vision to accomplish their mission. This book give us a reality of all the things that are important to keep two people together beyond love. Because yes love is never enough to stay somewhere, your worth at that place decides everything. Two people who have always known eachother get to know each other on the terms of responsiblities given to them by their love. And the biggest of them is, to be there for eachother. Only some know to prove it,while others simple know to speak it. With life's adversities two people figure it out to make it possible through every possible way they find.And yes that's what love is,never giving upon eachother. The main aim of this book is to reach all the people who are waiting,struggling or have decided not to fall ever again,that love is the kind that makes you the happiest and saddest person once at a time.With the right one who is meant to be yours truly,every situations can be dealt with. The word long distance seems so long,but is the most closest thing that one could ever experience in their life.The author believes that if you've survived a LDR then there's nothing that you cannot achieve.Hope you'll find this one,relating to the one and only of your life.

Acknowledgements

I would like to thank Tahir Khan in the first place for being a true motivator when it came to talking about publishing the copies of my first book.I think today is the day where you'll be proud of me after these years.A true companion is always the one who comes to your mind first and yes miles away but always in my heart Shivanjali Pathak how do i even thank you for being a friend that proves every definition of being a partner in crime.I think the first overviewers are ones who we really trust the most and yes that's you Parth Sachdeva from being my senior to being my shadow,my true inspiration.My life would have always been incomplete if Anant wouldn't have come to bring in the magic of acceptances and the act of letting go things.Risha Sudarshan,isn't it like your dream coming true that you desperately wanted me to do,thank you for igniting that fire in me.I have always met my inspiration at the most unexpected time of my life and there it goes to the two doctors who have just changed my vision at looking things,Dr.Preeti Sharma and Dr.Neetu,I can never thank you enough for all the time you've just made me realize that how bold it is to stand alone bleeding while healing others.To everyone out there reading this,a big thank you to you too for giving this book a chance and your precious time to it.

Prologue

The choices choosen by you can be wrong but love can never be.Love doesn't always have to perfect all it needs to be is true.No matter where you go,true love will always find its way to you.Distance is just a small word when someone means so much to you.To every starting there's an ending too and endings doesn't have to be happy or sad,all they need to be is satisfactory.Because that's what the heart wants and if that doesn't happen then the cages of memories will cage you just like the emotional strings that have already been your controller. With a hope of finding someone who will truly belong to us we keep moving forward in our life. Not every door that's closed is locked, sometimes all you need to do is just push them,to be at the place where you deserve to be the most.

CHAPTER ONE

The contagious smile

Her eyes were searching everywhere to capture the most beautiful shot of her favorite city which she visited after 10 years of her job.With a hope that someone who meant so much to her in the past will reply to her even in the present.And she posted the story with that faith she had in him years earlier.After she returned to her house with lots of bags filled her choices and different shades,a notification popped at her screen.Even the stars were jealous of that sparkle in her eyes and she knew that they'll be meeting very soon."How come you're here?" he replied to her story,with a smile she said,how can I be far away from the place where I am supposed to be? And suddenly things have started between them,the things that were always meant to be happening but the timings were never right,may be this meeting was an indication of things that were going to start without any imaginations.She slept with dreams that already were going to turn into her reality but then there was a doubt of whether she is going to hurt somebody to whom her heart belonged at some point of her childhood.And yes she was thinking about Tanmay,the one who made her believe in love and the one who made her believe in betrayal too.She wanted to get rid of every feeling that was associated with him,but was unable to do that because something from the past was holding her just too tightly and she fell asleep with the thought that would it be right to make a place in Tanmay's best friend's life.The next morning she had that smile that was lost somewhere in the deep past that she was afraid to dig into,and yes it was from the one she was falling for,PJ she always called him by this cute nickname,and he asked her out to which she couldn't deny meeting him for the very first in person.Though there were 2 hours in their meeting but that not getting late in the first meeting showed everything that she was hiding from her too.She left her house to the place he was going to pick her up,with the wind swinging over her face,the sunshine giving a blonde touch to her wet hair,with curious eyes she looked for him,and yes he was there looking for her too.From a mile among the traffic he found her,their eyes met and their lips shared that smile that one shares when they meet after so long of knowing eachother.That adrenaline rush was seen in both of their faces,but yes that moment of glance was really a sparkling one.Some meetings are just like some unexpected greetings that one get to experience in their lifetime.And yes there are some people in our life to whom we can share a shoulder with no chance of any doubts.He was that person to her.They reached out to the ghats of ganges where all they could hear was deep silence of the things that happened in the past,and then she said PJ to which he replied yes my MJ and both of their eyes were just struck at eachother,though their lips didn't state any word but their eyes spoke everything that was important to be shared at that moment.And that deep silence was gone when he said,so how're you Manvi Joshi?All she wanted at that moment was to hug him tight and also shout like a real angry pal,Mr.Pranay Jain I am just the same way after

Tanmay left,she answered him with a smile.Tanmay was the real person because of whom two estranged good friends could meet after years of their friendship.Every kind of relationship has to go through different changes,but that doesn't make any of them a weak one,because whatever happens,happens for a reason and that reason can be discovered in any of the seasons with all of your acceptances and braveness.

CHAPTER TWO

The space between

There was something different in the morning after the last night they met eachother.There was a feeling of nothing has changed but it felt like something has definitely changed.The first question that crossed her mind was,does Tanmay know about my meeting with Pranay,should i text him if he knows or should i text PJ and ask if he knows that.But then its truly said people with whom you're attached get to know your gut feelings and then you may call it telepathy later.The text was from PJ,Manvi are you free just wanted to have a conversation about what happened the previous day!This didnt seem right to her and she replied yeahh sure!And the conversation went like

PJ: Do you know that Tanmay saw us together at the ghat we were at yesterday?

MJ: No,but whats the big deal about it,do you mind him knowing that?

PJ: You know i really dont care about what anyone else saw or talks about if it doesnt bother you,it doesnt bother me,simple.And yes if anyone says anything just confirm from me in first place thats the only reassurance i need from you and our friendship.

MJ: You know this is what i love that most about you,that you're just brutaly honest and i am brutaly too naive for this world.

PJ: Thats why now when i have got you,I want to keep you with all of my efforts that are needed to be a part of our thing!

MJ: Our thing???

PJ: Umm I simply mean't our friendship.Gtg bye! (Manvi hated to leave the conversations in between but then it was for the sake of her PJ)

MJ: Hmm bye!

Somewhere or the other Manvi had already understood what was the void that was between both of them but all she wanted to believe was in the present.That space between them made her feel like there's a lot to be known before entering a new chapter but there was a hope to make that chapter the best chapter of her life.She didn't knew which way to go,but she definitely knew how to go when the choices are been clear to her.

CHAPTER THREE

Flashbacks

Life is just never easy for some people, all of the differences in their life are created by their perspective of survival in the extremes. So was Manvi's life, just like the love that's said to be eternal in this world similarly her pain was. But to suffer was a choice,which she always hated to choose. She always believed in living in the moments because all we have today is just today. No one has ever seen even the next moments of the upcoming days so why not to indulge all of yourself into what you have today in your hands. Coming from a past that was so brutal and the reality that always stabbed her back all she had was her acceptances and her bold faith in a happy future that she will create for herself and for a lot of them like her. Nothing could ever shake her down from the moment she lost her mother and being tortured mentally by her father. There are some things that happen to some certain people because they are the most capable ones for handling that particular thing and yes with all of that boldness, experience and heartbreaks they lead a life beyond every happiness and love. When Manvi was 11, when she lost her mother due to cardiac arrest, she was naïve then so couldn't dig into the roots of what actually triggered this to happen. Her parents were never that ideal ones that seem to be happily married all they cursed was just each other. And being raised in such a house had definitely raised insecurities in that little girl's mind, that she even started doubting what real happiness feels like. One day after she returned to her house after her schooling was over, all she could find was bottles and blood over the whole house. She wondered what next life has to teach her and then there was her father behind her with a plate full of biryani that she loved when her mom used to make her favourite food of all time. She held that plate,and then all she could feel was that numbness in her heart and that choking over her throat.She wanted to just cry out badly not because her mom was not there but because she's not independent and has nothing that can help her out in moving out from her own house. A house is never build up by the 6pillars attached to the ceiling of the roof but it's build up by the people living inside with harmony and love. Everytime she used to figure out everything that she can possibly do and be on her knees but all she got was the will to accept every suffering that was thrown to her at every stage of her life.

Manvi are you even listening to what I am saying to you? A voice hit her ears but she was just lost somewhere else. MJ? hmm, a voice whispered. Where were you Manvi? – PJ asked her, I was just thinking about how can I possibly help you out with it.Are you sure? Yeah I am. There are some moments in our life that return to us in order to give us a reality check of how stronger we've become. But no matter how stronger we are, there are something's that we cannot erase, just like the flashbacks of the past. That keeps showering to us at some certain intervals of our life. Manvi was so lost in her own story that she couldn't even think about what her PJ has even told her. Pranay wanted Manvi to be part of his survival, but he was unaware of the battle that she was still fighting from since her childhood. Some wounds are curable while some of them just increase after digging more into them. And she just went off without a bye!

CHAPTER FOUR

The home date

Pranay had already sense the changes that were seen in Manvi because of the last night. But was clueless about what could change her mood and give her relief at present.He knew that she would deny going out with him but he was also aware of the fact that she can't deny anyone at her home.So he took off his bike keys and went to her place to surprise her with favourite thing. Tringggggggg! The bell rang and Manvi came running to the door as her parcel was to arrive today. The moment she saw him,she looked at her dress and ran to her room to change her clothes.Pranay always loved to see her in red and he couldn't take off his eyes from her,hii Manvi how're you? PJ how are you here? You didn't even inform me before coming.Is there anything so urgent? I don't need any occassion to meet my MJ and she was left blushing after listening to this. So what made you come to see me off she asked him, Pranay wanted to discuss about the last night but he felt that this isn't the right time to ask her anything. Just nothing I simply wanted to spend time with you and see what I bought for you, your most favourite thing, Ice-cream. Meanwhile Manvi felt all of this as a dream because she has never got anything perfect in her life and when the perfect thing is happening, she's unable to trust it. They sat together and shared their black currents, with the currents flowing inside them as hormones. Manvi suddenly looked at his eyes, and Pranay realized that she wanted to share something but he truly respected her feelings so he didn't insist her and choose to understand her in a very better way. There are some special ones in our life to whom we may not say a word but their hearts definitely reach out to all the feelings and words we are stuck with. Pranay was that person to her who always knew how to uplift her mood, how to be there for her and definitely how to love her the right way. The only thing that was needed to make all of this happen was the right time.

CHAPTER FIVE

The first call

It was 7 in the morning where Pranay received a call, Sir do you know who Manvi Joshi is? He replied yes she's my friend, what happended to her? We really want you to reach here soon at 77/2 Dwarka road, near children's hospital. She's in emergency. Pranay couldn't bear this news and all he was left with was the tears and the memories that they created together in this lesser time. Pranay rushed out of his house to save the love of his life. He reached at the destination where he was called to but he couldn't find anyone out there.He was trying to call that number too but there was immense silence over the street. Pranay noticed someone coming from far away but he couldn't recognize. The wind was blowing and the sun was glancing Pranay didn't knew what to do further, he tried calling Manvi but then her phone was switched off. A voice from behind was heard, he turned back and then couldn't stop starting at the person he just saw. She was Satakshi Gupta, Pranay's ex. Hi Pranay how have you been these days without me? She asked him. Her attitude was her biggest problem that led to many unsuccessful relationship in her life. Pranay smiled at her and said nothing just looking out for someone who is in need of help. Manvi? and Pranay was shocked how come she knew about her! Who's she? - Pranay asked her. To which she replied the girl you're approaching and the girl who's fighting between her life and her death. This sentence killed Pranay from inside,all he wished for was to be with his MJ. Can you please tell me where she is recently? he begged to her and Satakshi was smiling out there. Definitely, I will be the only reason to take you there but all you need to do is sign some of the contracts so that I get some share in your professional business too. Pranay had no choice to sign them and he did, just for his MJ. Satakshi drove him to Menakshi Hospital that was just next 3 lanes and he went running to the room 208 of the third floor. The moment he saw MJ over the drips of blood, tears fell from his eyes. But he also saw somebody whom he never wanted to be around Manvi again after all the sufferings that were offered by him to his MJ. That broke him more and that's where the life played its real game.

Game changer

And yes Tanmay was there holding out her hand and when he saw Pranay approaching he started talking about the good old times that they both spend with eachother. Pranay was already broken so much that he was unable to decide what would be the best for him and his MJ. The doctors came in and happily said that Manvi is good at healing, so you'll be able to take her home. But take care of not stressing her because already she had some injury earlier. Pranay was shocked listening to this, and he wondered is there anything that this girl hasn't experienced? I want to be her shadow so that everything that comes to her meets me first in place he whispered to himself. Manvi reached out to Pranay and asked her to take her home back. Seeing Tanmay in her room made her forget about everything, a flashback of everything came forth her. Tanmay came to her and said Manvi, you don't even know what Pranay was doing while you were here. He came off with Satakshi, Manvi seemed clueless and she asked who? Tanmay said, his first love. This past would definitely change out both of their future only if they choose to stick out with it. Manvi asked Pranay if that was true? And he stood silent. Manvi with drips over her wrists walked out with tears in her eyes and wondered what's always wrong with me. Pranay came running to her and said that he can explain but Manvi was not in condition to hear him out at this moment. She believed in him, but also couldn't resist the reality that was thrown infront of her. Pranay drove her home and said Manvi can I stay with you so that I can help you out with everything you want. Manvi didn't react to anything that he said to her. And she went off with just one thought what if this was our last meet. She never wanted to be apart from him but she also didn't wanted to come between two people who loved eachother in the past and were separated because of some troubles. Manvi stood strong but not from inside. She wanted to tell him that today in the morning she was coming to his place to give him something, but then this thing happened. And changed a lot of things that were about to happen.

CHAPTER SEVEN

Chocolate

After the meeting that had shaken their belief system both
of them were in dilemma of what's next because none of
them wanted to loose each other after knowing that they
have got each other's back.She texted,PJ I bought
something for you yesterday but was so much lost in that
moment that it just skipped from my brain,can we meet
again?Soon the reply came with an emoji ? as if her PJ
was hoping to see his MJ again because of her gazing eyes
that allow him to drown in them as if all that moment is
forever,but somewhere both of them knew that they had
less time to spare with eachother.Manvi always knew that
her efforts would never go unnoticed in his case.She wore
a check lavender top wearing a plated ponytail,with dark
kajal over her eyes and a nude shade over her lips and
was smiling looking at herself,and a voice note appeared
on her screen,MJ MAI AAGYA HUN NEECHE AUR KITNA
TAIYAAR HOGII!!!!!(MJ I have come outside your house
please don't be late because of your getting rcady
skllls).Her cheeks turned red when she saw him over black
shirt,long back she once said to him that black suits you
really well,and see how much he remembered in detail.Her
hands were searching for something inside her purse and a
bournville came in her hand and she said,PJ Thank You for

always being there for me whenever I just needed someone to be beside me,thank you for all of the days where you stood for me when tanmay left me in the middle.I never knew that we'll be meeting but now when its happening I would really want to thank you from the core of my heart,you'll never know how important you were to me PJ after you stopped talking to me when tanmay asked you to do so,I was completely shattered and that made me question all of the moments I've shared with you in video calls.Pranay was silent and numb at the same time but he knew what he has to say,he shook his head and took that chocolate from her,held her hand firmly and pulled her outwards himself.With tears in his eyes and her head over his chest,he whispered MJ I know I have just done wrong with you after knowing how wrong that phase was for you,but now I want to compensate everything that went wrong by making it right,just by being beside you.And Manvi had a bad outbreak hugging him even more tighter.And she whispered,"Promise me that that you'll always stay my PJ while I'll always stay your MJ."And that smile with Pranay's numbness said it all,because words mean so little when someone means so much to you.The darkness has brought two people together with a hope that,the light that enters today,will be the brightness that outshines tomorrow. remembering this Manvi went to her house with a relief that the chocolate she bought for him,is with him,the actual one for whom it was meant to be.

CHAPTER EIGHT

Night changes

Pranay was over-whelmed by whatever happened the previous day. But was completely shaken by the past days, they were just too harsh over him. But if one gets a choice here to escape such days then definitely this world would have been a more happier place than it is today. Riyansh was the only friend of Pranay that knew about his feelings for Manvi, its truly said that the world will always feel your love, except for the person who is your world, and thats why the proving and re-assuring concept was build up by great lovers of this world. Pranay talked to Riyansh about everything that happened in the past days about the deal with Satakshi that he had to sign in order to be with Manvi soon. He didn't seem to be hearing all this but a good friend knows every good that you deserve in your life. He asked Pranay to confess his love to Manvi and let destiny decide where to take you guys, with loyalty and understanding every realtionship can be made perfect,only if one decides to never quit over them. Many of them know this, but only fewer can make this happen. Not everybody around you deserves a chanee to prove their love, but everyone around you should get a chance for the confessions of their feelings. Finally with a lot of courage Pranay dialled to her and was high on his nerves. HELLO!- MJ said, and Pranay was lost there only. I wanted to ask is everything okay,do you need something,just tell me? - he replied to her. No, I am totally fine after giving you the thing that was meant for you, and my health is improving so thank you for your concern. There was a big silence after she said this, Manvi do you know why I came to the hospital with Satakshi? She said, Pranay I trust you and there's no past that can make me feel insecure when I know I am well secured in my present. And this maturity of her made Pranay fall in love with her even more. Now tell me the exact reason of calling me this late, she added. Umm actually there was a confession that I really want to make before I loose you to someone else,she was blushing behind the call but showed her strictness by saying go ahead MR.PJ. Manvi I really dont like to call you that because I want all of the rights to call you my one and only MJ [And here J stands for Jain not Joshi,he whispered to himself and smiled]. Manvi didn't know how to react to this but she said, PJ you are never loosing me,once you've got me,you've got me for forever. Also should I reply you with 'I LOVE YOU MORE' or something more cheesy than you said. And both of them giggled over the call. Some moments are worth capturing, only if we don't hold cameras in our hands but definitely in our eyes with that sparkle because of those moments.

CHAPTER NINE

December

Winters were the only reason that made Manvi Joshi so cold. Just like some people that crave for the sunshine amidst the coldest days of the year, she also craved for december to make her more and more bolder than ever. While the whole world prepares themselves for the new comings of new year and new things, Manvi prepares herself for new experiences and new pain. The most brutal moment of her years were always in december, but her most favourite. May be a lot of things change when you have the right ones beside you. And she had her PJ with her, always. Christmas was about to come and Manvi was about to leave for her official work city. So Pranay wanted the celebrations to be done before she goes to her place. He came to her house and hugged her.Everything was just magical in that moment,the bells around the doors, the red lights over the walls, the tree covered decors and her in that red santa cap. Pranay never wanted to be apart from that sparkle that her eyes radiate when they are together. And suddenly the song began, Dashing through the snow
In a one-horse open sleigh, Jingle bells, jingle bells,
Jingle all the way.
Oh what fun it is to ride
In a one-horse open sleigh, hey!

And Pranay grabbed her and starting dancing with her, that happiness was never seen over her face after her mom had left this world. A lot of people go through a lot of it but only some of them are able to deal with it. The christmas was spent beautifully with all the smiles that had the bruises of the past. And Manvi went to kitchen to arrange all the food items that she cooked for him over the dining. Pranay was in her room and he found a diary, he decided to not open. But he still did it. In order to help people out there we must be familiar with all of their past, so that their present can really be like a beautiful present. And the very first page stated about her mother, with a beautiful poetry that she wrote when she was not at home and her father treated her the wrong way.

Nobody like her: Mother
She accepts whatever you give her
Without making any choices
But doing many compromises
She lives a life not of her own will
But of others bills
She works all the 365 days
Including the leap year
But no one pays her
And no one respects her
All she does is for everyone
And none she does is for herself
She gives all of her happiness to her family
But gets nothing in return
She never expects anything
The only thing she does is accept everything
She never reveals her choices
But always listens to everyone's voices
When she's around there's a warmth that gathers us

And when she's far the eyes fill with tears
She gives a special place to her children in her heart
But never expects the same with her case
She believes in faults
But never blames by taunts
She gives hope to the hopeless
And love to heal the pain
But she isn't aware that her warmth heals everything
The touch of the soul
Gives peace to my heart
And her soothing voice
Melts my soul
All her beauty is captured
In her daughter's eye
And all her flaws have become a memory to cherish
Though she will be back after some days
But those some days feel like years to me
And I can't survive without her warmth or her presence
She does so much for us
But we never evaluate that by calculations
Instead we focus on what's left
And she's not someone who
Sacrifices her whole life to see that smile on her family's
faces
But she's my mother
For whom I felt today
When she left me alone
To make me more capable of things
And I realized what our moms do for us and how much I
love her
These distances told me the real
Value of you today in my life
But I am thankful to that because if this moment would

not have come today then I would have never realized how much I love you and what's your importance in my life
#I love you mom

And Pranay wanted to give her every happiness that she was deprived of in her childhood. Manvi came to her room and saw him holding that diary and said, don't ever touch my things before asking me! Pranay said MJ now that I am with you, you don't have to hide anything because once you've got me,you've got me for forever, he added her lines. And tears fell from her eyes and she hugged him with no air gaps between them. All that one could ever need in their lifetime is a loyal company of someone who is willing to stay in the odds as well as in the evens.

CHAPTER TEN

The mile closer rituals

The flight was late 4hours due to some climatic reasons. And all Manvi was thinking about was how beautiful that last night was spend with the love of her life. Everyone deserves to be that happy atleast with the ones they are meant to be truly. But the time period of waiting and searching for them really sucks. And yes Dhara was waiting for her best friend desperately. When she saw Manvi approaching,all she shouted was PJ KI DULHAN DOST KO BHOOL GYI KYA [Wife of Pranay did you even forgot your best friend,after meeting the love of your life] Manvi came running to her and said I missed you so much bro. This bro code never ends if started with the true ones. She texted her PJ that she has reached out safely. So the official sucking life was back again. No matter where ever you go but you will always have to return back to the places where you're needed the most. All that one needs after that tiring day is that call from the person with whom we are truly connected to, and yes it was heer PJ's call to her. Helllllloooooo PJ, didn't you miss me the whole day? And he was numb there. What happened Pranay? she asked him. Manvi I want to marry you, because I really can't be without you. A lot has already happened and I can't see myself without your presence. Okay so i have an idea, lets get married. Are you serious MJ ? he asked her. Ofcourse,darling. So its like we'll do 7promises to eachother according to the hindu culture, Qabool hai thrice according to the muslim culture and according to the christainity we'll kiss eachother and then we'll be finally married. You are the one I was always waiting for,my sweetheart. And the promises went like.

PROMISE 1 BY Manvi : I'll always be there for you no matter what.

PROMISE 2 BY Pranay : I'll always support you in your good and bad times

PROMISE 3 BY Manvi : I'll always respect your family.

PROMISE 4 BY Pranay : I'll always trust you no matter what comes infront of me.

PROMISE 5 BY Manvi : You will always be my priority after my duty.

PROMISE 6 BY Pranay : I'll never let us apart,my efforts will be constant for you.

PROMISE 7 BY Manvi : I'll always try my best to understand you.

Let's come to the next ritual, Manvi added.

So MR.Pranay Jain kya apko niqah qabool hai? [do you agree onto marrying her] Qabool hai, Qabool hai , Qabool hai. [YES,YES AND YES]

Manvi kya apko niqah qabool hai? [do you agree onto marrying him] Qabool hai, Qabool hai , Qabool hai. [YES,YES AND YES]

Think again otherwise a girl will always be hanging over your head for the rest of your life MR.Jain, she said. I would love to be that guy ma'am, he added.

So the final one

You say- Manvi said

No,girls first - Pranay said

And   together   they   said
MUUUUUUAAAAAAAAAHHHHHHH!

So the virtual wedding is done,when should I be coming to your house? Pranay asked mockingly. TOMORROW,she replied. Are you serious girl? YES. And that happiness just reached the level above the sky and deeper than the oceans

.

CHAPTER ELEVEN

The ethnics

And finally the most awaited day of their love story has arrived.No story is written perfect from the heaven,but its made perfect in its hell of the days with constant efforts,understanding and love that grows daily towards each other.Today was the day her PJ was to be introduced as MR.Pranay Jain to her family,nothing can be more exciting and scaring than the day of the proposal.The morning was horrible for Pranay and he got late because of continuously talking over the video call last night.He reached out to Manvi but her phone was dead.All that came to his mind was it's just okay,the starting is just bad,I'll have to reach through out the end with struggles all around my way so that I don't disappoint my MJ and be able to keep my promises.And he started getting ready,and got a call from Manvi.With sleepy voice Manvi said,Hello Darling what's up? Manvi do you know what day is today?He shouted.Yes baby I know its sunday,and sunday is funday.Manvi I am about to reach your house in 30mins I want you to be ready.And she got up in a hurry and said don't just joke around me man!Is that day really today?Yes,my MJ.And this melted her heart,and she went running to her dad and stood quite after seeing her.Her dad was a well disciplined man but she also knew how to tackle him.

Daddy,someone is coming to meet you! - She said

Who manvi? - Her dad replied

Someone you know but just not in that way... - She replied

Okay let me also see in what way people are wanting to meet me - He replied to her in his own mocking way

Meanwhile,her phone was ringing and she wondered how come PJ is just so quick! But no everytime your loved ones are not supposed to surprise you,so yeah another surprises are from your offices.That are desperately waiting for your presence with absence of your brain.And she said nooooo,not today.Though it stated emergency but this was supposed to be her big day.But it was her work and she cannot escape that at any cost.She texted to PJ that she wont be able to meet in her house,so whatever that's gonna happen will be in the hands of him.This text made him nervous,but understandable of the fact that you can't escape your life's first priority,your work.

And Mr.Pranay Jain entered her house while everyone in the family was shocked to see him well dressed with flowers in his hands and visiting his best friend's house in formals.Her aunt asked him to come over and join the company of her strict father,but not that strict but still strict.

So Mr.Pranay Jain what made you come here? - Her father asked (How can the daughter be so alike to her father,this is exactly what she already prepared me for)

Sir,I just wanted to meet Manvi so that I can confess my feelings for her.- PJ replied in a decent manner.

She's not home,and what feelings? - Her father questioned him raising his eyebrows

If she's not here then its okay but being her family you can truly connect to what I will tell to you people and also you may convey to her in a more better way than I could ever - PJ said this with shaking nerves

Okay tell - Her father insisted

Sir,I've known your daughter for almost 20 years,been her friend since then and loved her since 10years and the remaining ones I wanna spend with her.Because she's the one that belongs to me- PJ replied to her father with glance of confidence in his eyes truly speaking out.

But how are you the one that belongs to her? - Her father cross-questioned him

I know I am not but ever since I have met her I am trying to be the one who deserves her,the one who truly protects her,the one who respects her,and the one who loves her just like her father does. - PJ has stole her dad's heart.

I don't know if you are really the one for my daughter through all of the words you've said,but all I know for sure is the one who never gets rid of trying,of improving and of accepting is the one for my daughter.And I see that person in you.But as its my daughter's proposal, I want it to be a surprise for her,so ignore her while she's off to work and call your parents too so that we surprise her all together - Her father said this with a hidden smile over his face.

All that PJ wanted to do at that moment was to call his lady and just say that you're officially mine.But her father was the real king this time.So yes his rules.

*************After 9 hours**************

Yashu did PJ come to the house? - Manvi shouted,but there was absolute silence.

please pick up the phone PJ,where are you man! - Again there was no response.

Manvi went to the kitchen and opened the fridge to have some ice-tea to soothe her brain and then think about what's next.And she read a note that stated: PLEASE COME

TO THE TERRACE,ITS EMERGENCY!

She ran in hurry with faster heartbeats all she could see was immense darkness,that made her go nuts. Dad where are you? Please tell me pleaseeeee,and she outbursted standing there.

AND THE LIGHTS TURNED ON

And there was her PJ holding a ring for her asking her out so,MISS MANVI JOSHI will you be my MRS.MANVI PRANAY JAIN.And she hugged him tightly and cried out more louder.And then both the families came out clapping with rose showers and she wondered where could she ever get someone best than her PJ,definitely never in any new life because she wanted to live every life in these moments being beside him.

Later on Manvi realized that when they had their first call,PJ asked her about her ideal wedding proposal,this is how exactly she told him,and years later this is how exactly he proved to her that not everyone is meant to stay in your life,some of them are meant to depart so that the one that truly deserve you,gets you.And this time they had their rituals being miles closer with their favourite ethnics in their favourite month,december.

The Reality

This is a story of two people who have met eachother after seeing life's every shade. And they decide to spend the next years of every shade that come to them, together. The main purpose to write this book was to fulfill the dreams of a lover,no body is ideal because then partners would have no meaning. There are some secrets that I would want to reveal, firstly with the cover page. The black and white cover page indicates the profession of the girl and boy,one as a doctor and one as a lawyer respectively. There are 11 chapters in this book, that indicates the total months they have spend together,the most beautiful time of their entire life.

And a voice whispered in my ears,"where do we go from here?" TO ALL THE PLACES THAT HAVE OUR FOOT PRINTS EMBEDDED

-she replied